In loving memory of my abuelas,
Delia Ibañez and Benita Elena Miranda—Y.S.M.

For my madar bozorg,
Soghra—K.A.

Library of Congress Control Number: 2020941018
ISBN 978-0-06-283995-4

The artist used scanned in pencil line, scanned in textures and Photoshop to
create the digital illustrations for this book. Typography by Erica De Chavez.
20 21 22 23 24 RTLO 10 9 8 7 6 5 4 3 2 1 ❖ First Edition

What Will You Be?

by Yamile Saied Méndez illustrated by Kate Alizadeh

HARPER
An Imprint of HarperCollinsPublishers

"**W**hat will you be when you grow up?" they ask.

"Your mom's this. Your dad's that.
It's never too soon to dream of
what *you* will become."

I don't have to think much.

"When I grow up.
I will be an . . . astronaut!

A unicorn,

or . . . a clown."

"No, what will you *really* be?" they insist.

I ask Abuela because
she has been everything
under the Sun and the Moon.

She says she's still figuring out what to be when *she* grows up.

"Abuela, when I grow up, what will I be?"

Abuela pauses her work.
Bright colors drip from her paintbrush.
She looks at the splatter on the floor
as if she's reading my future.

When she looks at me, her eyes sparkle. "You know yourself the best, mi amor," she says. "Child, what will you be?"

Nothing comes to mind.

Abuela points to my heart and says, "Listen."

I close my eyes, so I can hear the words no ear can catch.
Inside me, underneath the rhythm of the
drumming, there's a quiet voice.

I ask softly,
"What will I be?"

The answers come fast
in a rush of colors and sounds.

I will be a builder.
I will mold the world in my hands
into homes of every shape.

Into havens with bookshelves
in every corner and a big kitchen where
all are welcome at the end of the day.

I will be a dreamer, finding shapes in the moving clouds.

I'll write and paint my dreams, and my words and pictures

will inspire others to tell their stories too.

I'm small, but I'm a warrior with my pen and brush!

of the lands where my roots were born.
My ancestors created roads where there were none.

Now I march ahead with their
strength to the stars for which I'm destined.
Who knows what roads are waiting for me?

When I grow up,
I will be a farmer.

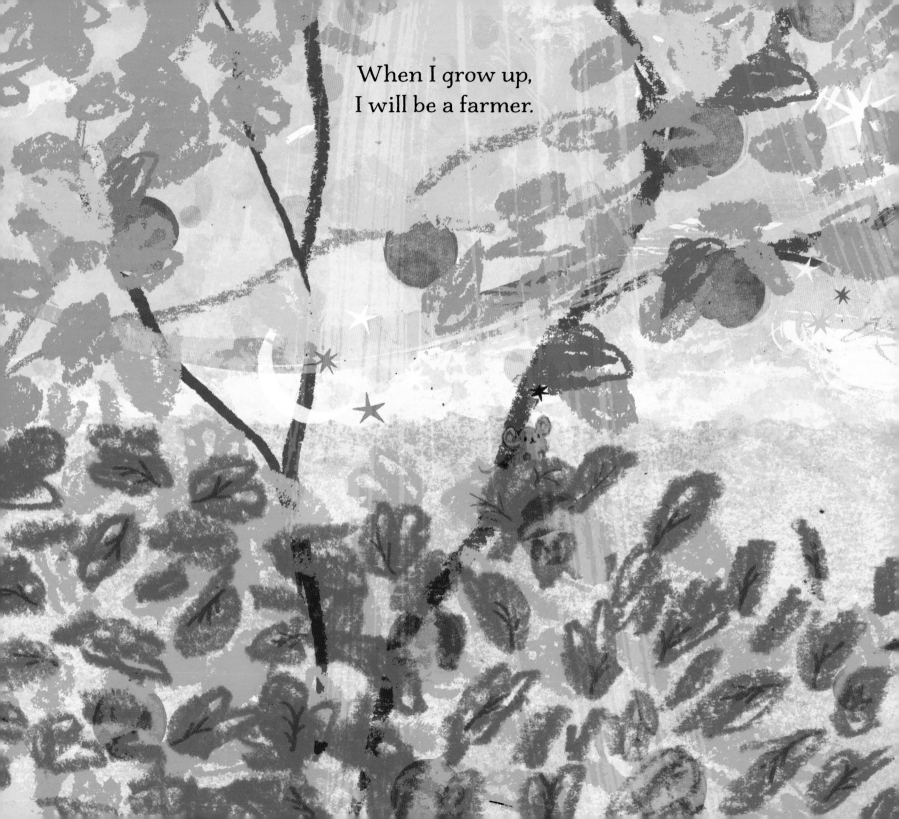

Planting wonder and change,
and harvesting the power and knowledge that
sprouted for those who dreamed before me.

Now with that power and knowledge,
I will be a healer of broken bones
and why not—even hearts.

A voice against injustice and hurt;
A mender of wrongs.

When I grow up, I'll be a student.
Looking inside myself and other people
to understand what makes each of us one
of a kind, all magical and different,
all needed and appreciated.

I'll also be a teacher and leader,
sharing my light even in the greatest darkness,

remembering that laughter is a universal language,
understood by young and old.

"Good job, my child," Abuela says,
"All these things you can be and more.
But remember, when a job is too big for little hands,
many hands can work miracles."

Abuela hands me her paintbrush and, with wonder,

I discover the way colors come alive on a blank canvas,

just for me.

When I grow up . . .

I will be me.